THE BARE

CHAMPION

By
Michael Gervais

Illustrated by
Cornelius Van Wright

STAR BRIGHT BOOKS
CAMBRIDGE, MASSACHUSETTS

Published in the United States of America by Star Bright Books, Inc. The name
Star Bright Books and the Star Bright Books logo are registered trademarks of
Star Bright Books, Inc. Please visit: www.starbrightbooks.com.
For bulk orders, please email: orders@starbrightbooks.com, or
call customer service at: (617) 354-1300.

Printed on paper from sustainable forests.

ISBN-13: 978-1-59572-705-3
Star Bright Books / MA / 00104150
Printed in Canada / Marquis / 0 9 8 7 6 5 4 3 2 1

Library of Congress Cataloging-in-Publication Data

Gervais, Michael.
 The barefoot champion / by Michael Gervais ; illustrated by Cornelius Van Wright.
     pages cm
 Summary: Convinced that expensive new shoes are his ticket to playing professional
basketball, a boy is stunned to find that he can be beaten by Mokey, a poor, younger
boy from Harlem who plays barefoot.
 ISBN 978-1-59572-705-3 (pbk. : alk. paper)
 [1. Basketball--Fiction. 2. Shoes--Fiction.] I. Van Wright, Cornelius, illustrator. II.
Title.
 PZ7.1.G475Bar 2015
 [E]--dc23
                              2015002164

"To my first class, my second graders, especially Jahki. What are you writing these days?"

— M.G.

This is the story of my All-Star shoes and the short life they lived on my size 9 feet.

This is the story of a barefoot champion.

CHAPTER ONE

The day I bought my Black and Red Double Dunks was the best (and worst) day of my life. My mama said they cost seven and a half months' allowance.

I said, "Mama, please! I'll be making more than seven and a half months' allowance in one minute when I become an NBA All-Star player!"

She giggled, like she always does. We walked to the Hoops on 125th Street, and Willy—that's what his name tag said—brought me a pair. I restrung them twice each, looked them over, every inch, tried them on five times, and then nodded to my mama.

This was *the* pair. This was the pair that would get me to the NBA.

Walking home, I already felt like a champion. My face was glowing like a flashlight in a blackout. Even Mr. Jones, who spends most of his days sitting on the stoop feeding lost pigeons, noticed something different about me.

"What are you thinking about, boy?" he yelled, grinning from ear to ear.

When I got to my apartment building, Mama gave me the keys. I let myself in and ran up the creaky steps, faster than that time I ran away from Mr. B.'s mean, dripping-mouth dog.

First floor . . . second floor . . . third floor . . . fourth floor . . . deep breath . . . finally, fifth floor.

I slipped into my apartment, opened the box, and there they were. I ripped off my torn, worn sneakers and slipped on my new shoes.

I stared down at them. My bedroom was

stuffy and sweat rained down my back, but when I put on my new shoes, I was cool . . . I was ice cold . . . I was All-Star. I was NBA. I made the same sound that Grandma makes when she drinks her iced tea on a hot day: "Ahhhhhh."

I threw down the empty box and slipped out of the apartment, leaving the door wide open, and ran right down the stairs. Fifth floor . . . fourth floor . . . third floor. . . second floor . . . deep breath. . . finally, first floor.

I almost zoomed right past my mama. She was still outside, talking to Auntie Kay, when she stopped me in my tracks.

"Meeting the boys at the court, Mama. I'll be home in time for dinner," I said. I threw her the keys.

"Be careful, baby," she said. "It'll be raining soon."

CHAPTER TWO

But I hardly heard Mama. Ever since I slipped on my new shoes, it was just me and my dream of becoming an NBA All-Star player.

I slowed down, and soon my walk turned into a strut, like slow motion. I didn't crack a smile. I didn't blink. I didn't turn my head.

Heads turned to *me*, and gravity took their eyes right down to my Black and Red heaven.

When I got to the courts, Jo, Skinny, and Chase were taking it easy in the heat.

"Hey, it's—" Jo's mouth dropped.

"What you got there?!" Chase asked in his squeaky-leaky voice with one eyebrow raised.

"Those shoes are HOT!"

"Wait, wait, wait!" Skinny said, coming in behind Jo and Chase. "Did you rob the Hoops? Tell the truth. Tell the truth now. I can see it in your eyes. Thief. I can smell it. Thief *all* over you." The boys and I laughed loud enough to send the pigeons flying.

"Gentlemen, I didn't rob anything. I stopped by the Hoops with my mama this morning. You're looking at *brand-new* Black and Red Double Dunks. All mine. Full price. That's right, boys. Take it in and think about it for a minute now."

"Those shoes are for champions!" Chase said, his eyes wide open, running his hand across my right shoe.

The whole time, Jo walked in circles around me, dribbling the big orange basketball. Then he stopped, standing in front of me. "Nah. I could still take you on the courts." He threw the ball at me . . .

I caught it in my chest and threw it right back at him, even harder.

"Oooooooooooooh," Skinny and Chase replied.

"Let's go. First one to five," I said. "You ain't got nothing on this All-Star."

"Oooooooooooooh," Skinny and Chase replied again, walking backward until their bottoms fell onto the empty bleachers.

I laughed. My friends are good for joking.

Five minutes later, *SWISH! SWISH! SWISH! SWISH! SWISH!* I beat Jo 5 to 0. I beat Skinny and Chase too.

Chase got so mad when I beat him. He threw the ball at the fence, and it bounced right back at him and hit him in the face. Skinny laughed so hard he fell to the concrete and shook around like a fish out of water.

"I am the champion!" I yelled, raising my

arms in the air. We were all laughing now.

"Watch out, Kobe," Chase yelled.

"Watch out, Paul Pierce," Skinny yelled.

"Watch out NEW YORK CITY!" I yelled, cupping my hands around my mouth.

My eyes caught someone standing outside the court fence. A shadow.

"Hey, you!" I yelled, pointing to the shadow. "Right now. First one to five. Let's GO!

"I am a champion! THE champion!" I yelled. "UNDEFEATED!"

CHAPTER THREE

"Let's head back to my apartment before it rains," Chase suggested. We turned around. Then we heard footsteps behind us. Our heads turned like mama's looking for the subway train.

Mokey Brown stepped out of the shadows . . . and into the courts.

Mokey was a short, skinny kid, half my size and two years younger. His arms and legs looked like jump ropes. He didn't say much, but when he did, his voice was real raspy, like when Grandpa's car won't start. *Rar! Rar!*

No one knew much about him, but one thing we did know was that he was the best basketball

player on the East Side of Harlem. Here on the West Side of 125th, we knew him as No Joke Moke. And he was no joke. His dribble was record speed. His layup—effortless. His slam dunk was in-the-clouds.

He walked toward me, slow like a snail, sly like a fox. "First one to five." He reached out his hand, waiting for me to shake on it. I would have just walked away, but then my eye caught sight of the mess near his ankles.

His shoes were so old that I didn't even recognize them. They looked like they were once blue, but now they were all shades of brown. The best part was, they were too small and the big toe on his left foot poked through. There was no way he could beat me with those shoes.

I looked at Mokey and scratched my chin like I've seen my daddy do when he was really thinking. "Deal," I said. I reached out to shake his dusty hand.

He grabbed my hand, pulled me toward him,

leaned in close to my ear, and whispered softly, "But if I win"—he scrunched his face and got in even closer—"I get your shoes."

I looked down at his rappy-snappy-I guess-you-could-call-those-shoes. There was no way he could beat me with those shoes.

"DEAL," I said. I backed up and bounced the ball right into him.

With the bounce of the ball, the game began. Jo, Skinny, and Chase stood by the fence, watching as I got in one shot after another. Four in a row. *SWISH! SWISH! SWISH! SWISH!*

Rain started to drop from the sky.

"Time out," Mokey snarled, catching his breath.

"No time outs," I said back.

But he didn't listen. Instead, he walked over to the bleachers and took off his shoes, one at a time. He threw them up on the bleachers. Bing, bang, BOOM—they bounced down one step at a time.

He stood in front of me, barefoot, ready to play.

"I play barefoot," he said, still catching his breath.

CHAPTER FOUR

Barefoot? I thought. I looked down at his sore, swollen, scratched-up feet. He couldn't beat me with no shoes.

"No Joke Moke has lost his mind," I heard Skinny mumble from the sidelines.

"Whatever you want, Jokey Mokey," I said, and the boys laughed.

With a bounce of the ball, the game started again. This time Jo, Skinny, and Chase watched as Mokey got in one shot after another. Four in a row. *SWISH! SWISH! SWISH! SWISH!*

"Time out!" I yelled. I needed to catch my breath. For the first time all day, I was nervous.

I looked down at my shoes. *All-Star,* I said to myself. You are an All-Star and he is barefoot! I took a few deep breaths and walked back on the court, ready to play.

"Game point," barked Mokey.

And then . . . *SWISH!*

And just like that, it started to pour buckets.

With that last swish, I fell onto the ground, my head in my hands. There was a lump inside my chest, like I had swallowed a rock the size of Manhattan. I lost. Everything I had heard about No Joke Moke was right. His dribble was record speed. His layup—effortless. His slam dunk was in-the-clouds. No one ever told me about his bare feet!

I could barely breathe. The rain kept coming.

When I finally looked up, Mokey was standing over me. He didn't have to say a word.

CHAPTER FIVE

I reached for my feet and slipped off my All-Star . . . full price . . . Black and Red . . . Double Dunks. I handed over my shoes, one at a time. It was like my dreams were slipping from my fingers. I desperately hoped he would hand them right back. But he didn't.

He took the shoes and, without saying a word, made his next move.

He swiftly tied the lace of the left shoe to the lace of the right shoe, and before I could blink . . . held the left shoe in his hand, wound up like he was pitching a fastball, the right shoe swinging around like a helicopter propeller, *whoosh, whoosh, whoosh,*

whoosh, aimed toward the sky, and let go.

The shoes flew through the rainy air and wrapped themselves around the telephone wire, like clothes on a line.

My jaw dropped. Mokey walked over to the bleachers, gathered up his old raggedy shoes, and left, without looking back.

Jo, Skinny, and Chase walked over and sat on the court next to me. We all sat staring up at my shoes for what felt like days as the rain poured down our faces, the lump in my chest even bigger now, my shoes, hanging from the telephone wires . . . perfectly still.

CHAPTER SIX

When it started to get dark, I picked up my soaking-wet self and began to walk home, barefoot. Tears fell down my face like the rain from the clouds . . . in buckets . . . as I lost sight of my shoes. The boys saw me crying but didn't say anything about it. They're good friends like that. No one said anything at all. They just walked right behind me the whole time and made sure I made it home.

When I got home, Mama took one look at me and my bare feet and said, "Stay by the door. I'll go get you some dry clothes."

Grandma was there too. She closed her eyes and shook her head.

"I knew those shoes were going to get you into trouble," she said. She ran her hand through my wet hair. "But don't you worry. I made your favorite for dinner, spaghetti and meatballs, Grandpa's recipe," and she smiled, like she always does.

CHAPTER SEVEN

I went back to the court a month later, and we just kept playing like nothing had ever happened. I never even looked up to see if my shoes were still there, but I heard that they looked like they were never coming down.

I never saw Mokey again, but I wonder. I wonder why he didn't keep the shoes. I wonder why Jo, Skinny, and Chase never spoke a word about what happened. I wonder why my mama was never mad.

I try to forget my Black and Red Double Dunks, and I have.

But I know one thing. I will never forget the Barefoot Champion.